Illustrations by Isabel Muñoz.

Written by Jane Kent.

Designed by Nick Ackland.

White Star Kids® is a registered trademark property of White Star s.r.l.

© 2018 White Star s.r.l.
Piazzale Luigi Cadorna, 6
20123 Milan, Italy
www.whitestar.it

Produced by i am a bookworm.

ISBN 978-88-544-1336-8
 2 3 4 5 6 23 22 21 20 19

Printed in Turkey

The life of Wolfgang Amadeus Mozart

WHITE STAR KIDS

My name is Wolfgang Amadeus Mozart, and I am a world famous musician and composer. I rose to fame in my early years, and then sadly I passed away at a very young age.

Follow my musical journey from talented child prodigy to one of the most celebrated composers of all time, whose work is still performed around the globe today.

Leopold

Maria

Nannerl

I was born on 27th January, 1756, in Salzburg, Austria. My parents were Leopold and Maria Pertl Mozart, and I had an older sister called Maria Anna who was nicknamed "Nannerl".

My father was a highly successful composer and violinist, and he was also the Assistant Concert Master at the Salzburg court. From a very early age, Nannerl and I were encouraged by him to take up music and, under his expert guidance, we both excelled. At the age of five, I created my first composition.

In 1762 when I was aged six and my sister aged eleven, our father took us to the court of Bavaria in Munich where we performed. We then travelled to the courts of Paris, London, The Hague and Zurich and were considered to be child prodigies.

Our European tour was long and exhausting.
During this time I met many talented
musicians, including Johann Christian
Bach, the youngest son of
Johann Sebastian Bach.
His work greatly influenced
my own.

My sister's musical career ended when she turned 18, as she had reached marriageable age. I was 13 and in December of 1769 my father and I set off for Italy, leaving Nannerl and mother at home. This time the tour lasted for two years, so that I could show off my talent to as many people as possible.

While we were in Rome, I heard a performance of "Miserere" by Gregorio Allegri in the Sistine Chapel. I was then able to write out the score from memory. I followed that by writing an opera for the court of Milan, called "Mitridate, re di Ponto". It was a success and lead to some commissions, including two more operas - "Ascanio in Alba" in 1771 and "Lucio Silla" in 1772.

When my father and I returned from Italy in March 1773, Hieronymus von Colloredo became the Prince-Archbishopric of Salzburg, replacing my father's benefactor Archbishop von Schrattenbach. He appointed me Assistant Concertmaster and this paid position offered me the opportunity to compose symphonies, string quartets, sonatas and serenades as well as operas.

I briefly worked on violin concertos, but in 1776 I developed an even greater passion for piano concertos. In 1777 when I was 21, I wrote "Piano Concerto Number 9 in E-flat major" which had three parts, or movements - Allegro, Andantino and Rondeau: Presto - and was a huge success.

Eventually I became restless in my role as Assistant Concertmaster in the city of Salzburg. In August 1777 I left to find more fulfilling employment, and because Archbishop von Colloredo would not grant my father permission to travel, this time my mother came with me to Mannheim, Paris and Munich.

I found and then lost several jobs, which unfortunately meant I began to run out of money and had to pawn some of my precious belongings. My mother became unwell on the trip and sadly passed away on 3rd July 1778. My father then secured a job as court organist back in Salzburg and I was glad to return.

Back in Salzburg I produced a series of works for the church, including the "Coronation Mass", and in 1781 I also composed another opera for Munich, "Ideomeneo". That March I was abruptly summoned to Vienna by Archbishop von Colloredo. Joseph II was ascending to the Austrian throne and the Archbishop was attending.

I was deeply offended by my treatment whilst there - it was as though I was a mere servant! - and this lead to a disagreement with the Archbishop. When I offered to resign, he refused to accept it and instead dismissed me. I decided to stay in Vienna and lived with friends at the home of Aloysia Weber whilst searching for work.

Luckily I got work quickly and easily in Vienna. I taught music, wrote music and played in concerts. I also found time to write another opera, which I called "Die Entführung aus dem Serail", or "The Abduction from the Seraglio". It was an immediate success, and my name started to become known across Europe.

On 4th August 1782 I married Aloysia Weber's daughter, Constanze. My father had disapproved of our relationship for some time, as he felt it would get in the way of my career, but we were in love and so he finally gave us his blessing. Constanze and I had two sons, Karl Thomas and Franz Xaver.

At the beginning of 1783 I was hugely inspired by Johannes Sebastian Bach and George Frederic Handel and so began to compose works in the Baroque style. Some of my later compositions that were influenced by this style include passages in "Die Zauberflote" - "The Magic Flute" - and the finale of "Symphony Number 41".

It was during this time that I met fellow composer Joseph Haydn and we soon became good friends who admired each other greatly. We often performed concerts with string quartets, and I wrote six quartets that I dedicated to him.

In 1784 I took part in 22 concerts in just five weeks. It was difficult to find available theater space to rent in Vienna at the time, and so I often had to book more unusual venues, from the largest room in an apartment building to the ballroom of an expensive restaurant. Many people attended my concerts, during this wonderful time for me, as I worked on perfecting my performance.

RESTAURANT

I met a Venetian composer and poet called Lorenzo Da Ponte at the end of 1785. Together, we worked on an opera called "The Marriage of Figaro" which premiered in 1786, first in Vienna and then in Prague. It was a huge success and so Da Ponte and I collaborated again.

Our opera "Don Giovanni" premiered in Prague in 1787 and was another hit. Both of these operas combine music and drama, and feature wicked aristocrats. They are still performed today and are considered to be two of my most important works.

Constanze and I lived a rather lavish lifestyle, paid for by my concerts. Our apartment was luxurious, we had servants and we sent our son Karl to an expensive boarding school. But by 1786 our extravagance had taken its toll and we were beginning to struggle financially.

I knew I needed to find stable employment, and hoped to find this through the court. Thankfully Emperor Joseph II made me his Chamber Composer at the end of 1787. It was a part time job and not very well paid, but it was a position of honour, helped to pay my debts and allowed me freedom to explore my own work.

But by the middle of the following year, Austria was at war and there was little call for musical performances. My family moved out of central Vienna to a small suburb called Alsergrund, where I hoped we could live more simply - and cheaply! Unfortunately that proved not to be the case, and I started borrowing money from my friends, which I repaid whenever I was able to perform in a concert.

I travelled to Leipzig, Berlin and Frankfurt to try to find work and earn money. I was unsuccessful and felt very down.

During 1790 and 1791 I became really productive again and wrote some of my best known works, including "Piano Concerto No. 27 in B-flat major" and "Clarinet Concerto in A-major". I performed a lot, regaining my fame and doing a little better financially.

However, I was not in the best of health by this time. In 1791 I was commissioned to produce an opera called "La Clemenza di Tito" - "The Clemency of Titus" - for the coronation of Leopold II as King of Bohemia. The timeframe was short and although I completed it in time for the September festivities, it was a huge struggle. Soon after I became bed-bound.

I succumbed to illness and died on 5th December 1791, at the very young age of 35. There has been much debate over the cause of my death, but officially it is recorded as being severe miliary fever which causes a millet seed-like skin rash.

Many people attended my memorial services and concerts, which were held in Vienna and Prague. Constanze found unpublished manuscripts that I had written and sold them, which helped her to pay off the debt I had left.

One thing I hope you will take from my story is that life is short, so it is important to make the most of every day. There is so much that you can accomplish when you set your mind - and your heart - to it. Follow your passion, aim for perfection and practice whenever you can. Music can bring so much joy to people and I am happy that audiences are still enjoying my work today.

Mozart was born in
Salzburg, Austria,
on 27th January.

1756

Mozart, aged six, performed with his sister
at the court of Bavaria in Munich.
They then went on a European tour.

1762

1761

He created his
first composition
at age five.

1769

Mozart went on
a two-year tour
of Italy with his
father. He heard
a performance
of "Miserere" by
Gregorio Allegri
and wrote out
the score from
memory.

ITALY

He wrote the opera
"Ascanio in Alba".

1771

Mozart travelled to Mannheim, Paris
and Munich with his mother.

1777

1773

1778

The Prince-Archbishopric of
Salzburg appointed Mozart as
Assistant Concertmaster.

His mother passed away and
so he returned to Salzburg.

Mozart was summoned to Vienna by Archbishop von Colloredo, but they fell out and Mozart was dismissed.

Mozart had a busy year, taking part in 22 concerts in just five weeks.

1781

1784

1782

1785

Mozart married Aloysia Weber's daughter, Constanze.

Kapellmeister Antonio Salieri collaborated with Mozart on a piece called "Per la ricuperata salute di Ofelia".

Mozart collaborated with Da Ponte on the opera "The Marriage of Figaro".

Mozart's family moved out of central Vienna to the suburb of Alsergrund.

1786

1788

1787

1791

Mozart was made Chamber Composer by Emperor Joseph II.

Mozart died on 5th December 1791, aged 35.

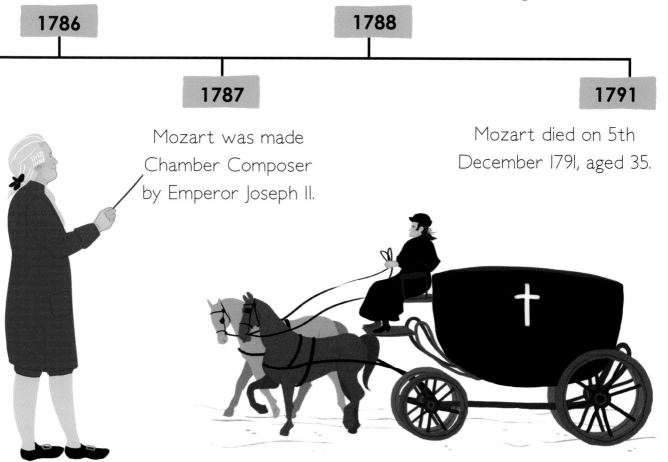

QUESTIONS

Q1. How old was Mozart when he created his first composition?

Q2. What was Mozart's sister Maria Anna's nickname?

Q3. Where did Mozart first hear a performance of "Miserere" by Gregorio Allegri?

Q4. Which two operas did Mozart collaborate with Lorenzo Da Ponte on?

Q5. What were the names of Mozart and Constanze Weber's two sons?

Q6. In just five weeks in 1784, how many concerts did Mozart take part in?

Q7. Where did the opera "The Marriage of Figaro" make its debut in 1786?

Q8. Who employed Mozart as Chamber Composer at the end of 1787?

Q9. Which suburb of Vienna did Mozart's family move to in 1788?

Q10. What illness is it believed Mozart died from?

ANSWERS

A1. 5 years old.

A2. Nannerl.

A3. In the Sistine Chapel.

A4. "The Marriage of Figaro" and "Don Giovanni".

A5. Karl Thomas and Franz Xaver.

A6. 22 concerts.

A7. Vienna and Prague.

A8. Emperor Joseph II.

A9. Alsergrund.

A10. Severe miliary fever.